DC BATMAN

5-MINUTE STORIES

BATMAN

5-MINUTE STORIES

Batman created by
Bob Kane with Bill Finger

Random House 🏠 New York

Published in the United States by Random House Children's Books, a division of Penguin Random House LLC, 1745 Broadway,
New York, NY 10019, and in Canada by Penguin Random House Canada Limited, Toronto. Random House and the colophon are registered
trademarks of Penguin Random House LLC.

The artwork that appears herein was originally published in *Batman: Fowl Play,* © 2013 by DC Comics; *Batman: Eternal Enemies,* © 2014 by
DC Comics; *Batman Versus The Riddler,* © 2014 by DC Comics; *Batman: Winter Wasteland,* © 2015 by DC Comics; *Batman: The Joker's Ice Scream,*
© 2015 by DC Comics; *5-Minute Batman Stories,* © 2015 by DC Comics; *I Am Batman,* © 2016 by DC Comics; and *Batman: Poison Ivy's Scare Fair,*
© 2017 by DC Comics.

rhcbooks.com

ISBN 978-0-593-12352-2 (trade) — ISBN 978-0-593-12353-9 (ebook)

MANUFACTURED IN CHINA

10 9 8 7 6 5 4 3 2 1

CONTENTS

BATMAN

IS THE DARK KNIGHT

As the young heir to the Wayne fortune, Bruce Wayne vowed to fight crime and injustice in Gotham City. He trained his body and mind to the peak of perfection and became Batman to frighten criminals. Armed with high-tech gadgets and powerful vehicles, Batman is known as the World's Greatest Detective. Along with his allies, Batman keeps Gotham City—and the world—safe from petty criminals and super-villains alike!

THE JOKER'S NIGHT OUT

One dark night in Gotham City, the Joker met with some of his criminal buddies. Around the table sat Harley Quinn, the Mad Hatter, and the sinister Scarecrow.

The Joker explained his plan to steal a lot of money . . . and just maybe bring down heroes Batman and Robin.

"Are you with me?" the Joker cackled. The other villains laughed and agreed to help.

The next night, as Batman and Robin
patrolled the city in the Batmobile,
a strange light shone in the sky.
   "That's not the Bat-Signal!"
exclaimed Robin.
   "Let's investigate," Batman replied.
He hit the gas, and the crime-fighting
machine roared off at top speed.

The Dynamic Duo quickly discovered the source of the light—it was coming from their friend Commissioner Gordon on the roof of police headquarters!

"He's wearing one of the Mad Hatter's mind-control hats," Batman said.

"I couldn't help myself," Commissioner Gordon said after Robin removed the sinister hat from his head. "But look—they left you a clue."

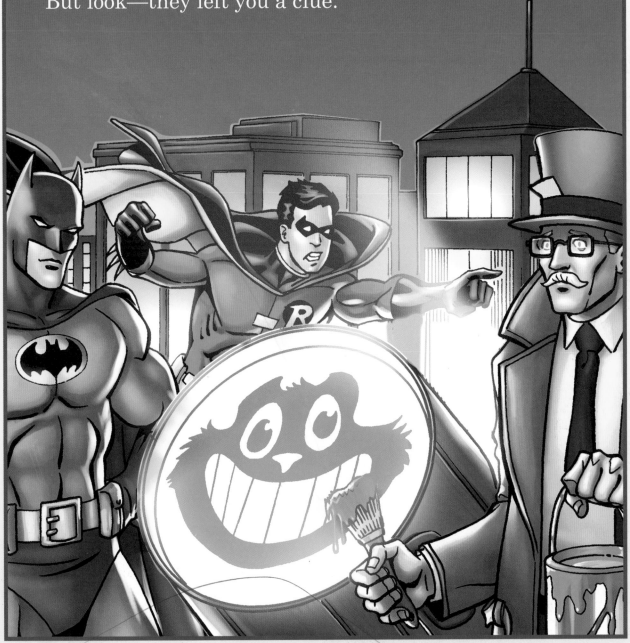

They looked at a message painted on the closest wall.

"What does it mean?" Robin asked, scratching his head.

"That's easy," Batman said. "Just look: 'a room of the house' is a hall, 'disguised as' means a costume, and 'fall and bounce' refers to a ball."

"Of course!" Robin cried. "It's the costume ball at City Hall!"

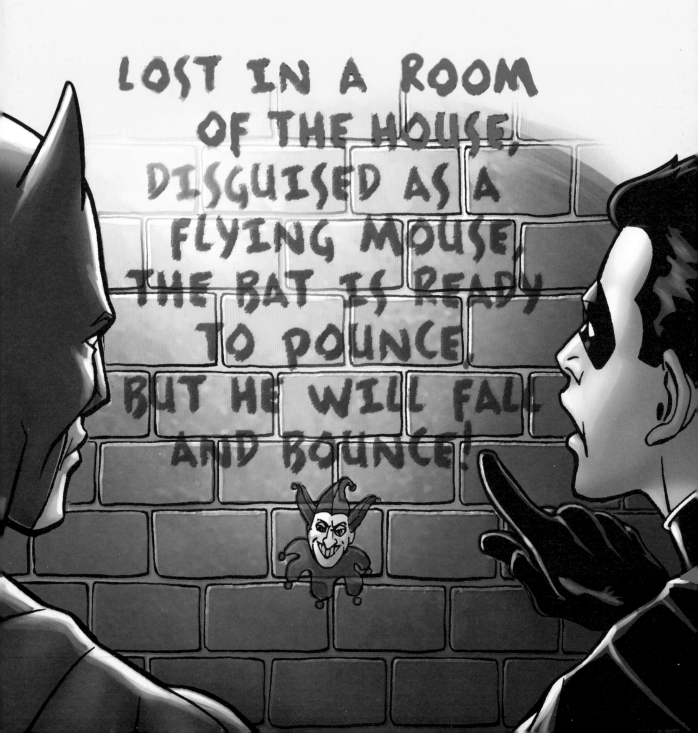

LOST IN A ROOM OF THE HOUSE, DISGUISED AS A FLYING MOUSE THE BAT IS READY TO POUNCE BUT HE WILL FALL AND BOUNCE!

Batman and Robin leaped into action.
In the rocket-powered Batmobile, they
would get to City Hall in no time!

Across town, the costume party, held to raise money for charity, was in full swing. Even the mayor was dressed up. He looked like a senator from ancient Rome.

The Joker and his criminal cronies arrived. They sprayed everyone with Fear Gas to make them too afraid of the villains to fight back. Then they set about taking the money raised by the party hosts, as well as everyone's valuables.

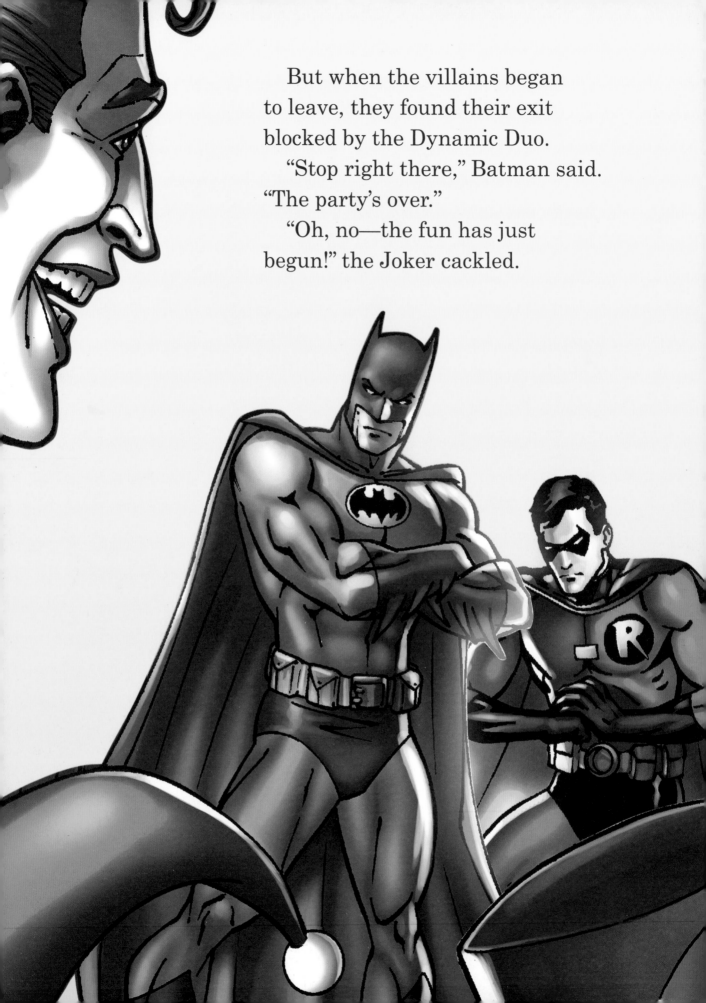

But when the villains began
to leave, they found their exit
blocked by the Dynamic Duo.

"Stop right there," Batman said.
"The party's over."

"Oh, no—the fun has just
begun!" the Joker cackled.

The Joker and Scarecrow tried to spray the Caped Crusader with Fear Gas, but Batman ducked out of the way and the two criminal creeps sprayed each other instead.

"PHEW—that's not funny!" the Joker said, gasping for breath.

"YUCK!" fumed the Scarecrow.

Then, with two quick karate moves, Batman took the fight right out of the Joker and Scarecrow. The Caped Crusader did not see that the Mad Hatter was trying to get in on the action.

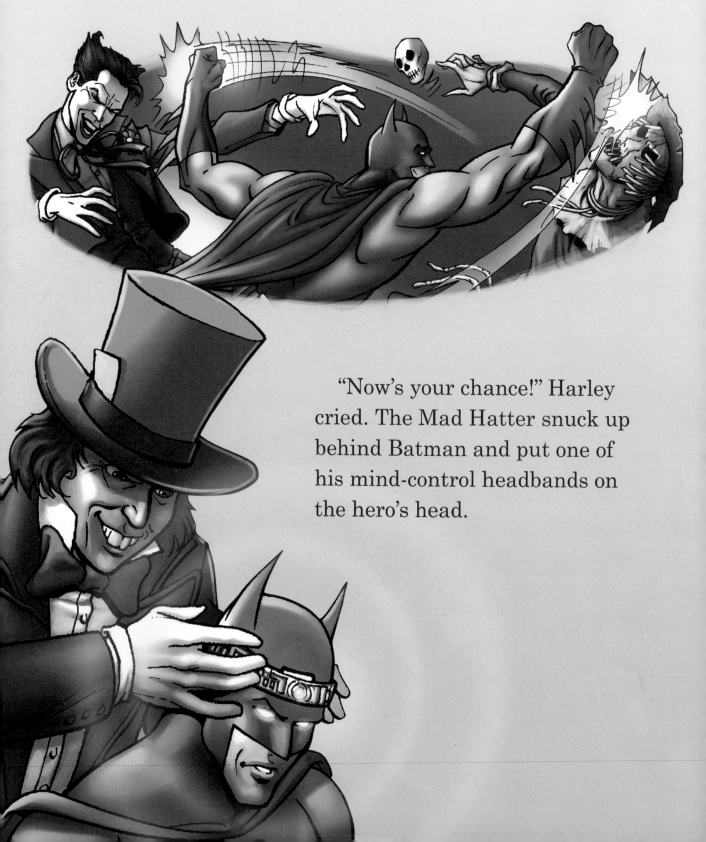

"Now's your chance!" Harley cried. The Mad Hatter snuck up behind Batman and put one of his mind-control headbands on the hero's head.

"Dispose of the Boy Wonder," the Mad Hatter commanded Batman.

The hero picked his partner up over his head. Batman's grip was too strong to break, so Robin thought quickly. He grabbed one of his Batarangs and hurled it.

THUNK! It hit the Mad Hatter and knocked the control device out of his hand, sending it spinning away.

Batman was free of the villain's power. He took the mind-control headband off and crushed it.

"Let's end this little get-together," Batman said to Robin.

"You got it, Batman," Robin replied, springing into action.

Robin saw Harley making a break for the exit. He grabbed Scarecrow and threw him across the room. The villain tumbled into Harley, stopping her as she tried to flee.

"It was fun while it lasted, but it looks like the *fun* is over," the Joker said, giggling. He grabbed the money and valuables and ran for the door.

"Let's pull the rug out from under this bumbling burglar," Batman said to Robin. With a good yank, they send the criminal clown falling face-first into a cake. SPLAT!

"We'll take it from here," said Commissioner Gordon after he and the police arrived to take the criminals away. "They can continue their night out in jail."

"Thank you," the mayor told Batman and Robin. "And everyone here agrees—you win the Best Costume prize. Congratulations!"

With the mayor and City Hall safe again,
the Dynamic Duo raced off into the night.

BIRDS OF A FEATHER

Valuable items were being stolen from people's homes all over Gotham City. At the location of each crime, Batman—the World's Greatest Detective—found a bird feather.

"This can't be a coincidence," he said, examining the latest feather.

Later, Bruce Wayne, Batman's alter ego, studied the clues in his private lab at his home, Wayne Manor.

His butler, Alfred, brought a news report to his attention. It seemed that birds all over the city weren't following their natural habits. Some were even missing!

"Interesting," said Bruce Wayne, rubbing his chin in thought. "I wonder if one of my old foes is up to no good. This sounds like the work of the—"

Suddenly, an alarm sounded. Bruce Wayne and Alfred raced upstairs. Through a broken window, they saw a large vulture flying away with an umbrella full of valuables in its talons.

"It got my cell phone," Wayne said, "but luckily, all my tech has tracking devices. Following that bird will be easy for Batman."

Bruce Wayne headed down the secret staircase that led to the Batcave.

"Alfred, warm up the Batplane. I think I'm going to need a bird's-eye view to solve this mystery."

"Right away, sir," Alfred replied.

Within minutes, Batman was roaring through the sky over Gotham City. The tracker was working perfectly—not that he needed it. It wasn't difficult to see where he needed to go. There were several birds circling a skyscraper, and more of them were coming from all directions. Each had an umbrella full of stolen items. As the birds landed, they crawled through a skylight that led to the Iceberg Lounge— hangout of notorious gangster the Penguin.

Batman slipped through the same skylight. He followed the sounds of birds squawking and chirping, and quickly located the cause of the current crime wave.

"Penguin! Just as I suspected," Batman said when he came face to face with the gangster.

"Who else could be behind such a *fowl* crime?" the villain replied with a laugh. "There's almost no place I can't get to with my fine-feathered friends!"

TWEEEEEET!

The Penguin blew a whistle and the birds attacked Batman.
"I've trained them to work for me," said the villain.

"I'm pretty sure it won't take much to convince them that you're a bad boss," Batman replied, pulling a Batarang from his Utility Belt.

The hero hurled the Batarang at a fire alarm. That
set off the sprinklers, which showered the birds with
cold water. The shock freed the birds from the Penguin's
control, and they flew toward the open skylight to freedom.
"Now it's your turn," Batman said, tackling the villain.

"I'm not quite so easy to cage, Batman!" Penguin snarled.
He flipped a switch on his umbrella and it turned into a rocket,
which shot him out of the Caped Crusader's reach.

Batman pulled a freeze grenade from his Utility Belt,
activated it with a touch of his thumb, and hurled it into the air.

POOF! The grenade went off, showering the flying felon with frost!

Batman called the authorities. Commissioner Gordon and the police arrived a few minutes later and found the Penguin already put on ice.

"Thanks to you, Batman," said the commissioner, "we not only have the Penguin, but we also have enough evidence to put him in a jail cell for a long time."

"He's the only bird I know of that shouldn't fly free," Batman replied.

NIGHT OF THE NINJAS

One night at the Gotham City Museum, a skylight shattered and ninjas leaped silently to the floor. Even the broken glass barely made a sound as it fell. They were on a mission . . . and it wasn't a good one.

A wealthy-looking man in fine clothing adorned with gold slipped in behind them and went to a display case. He broke the glass with his bare fist and pulled out an ancient scroll.

"At last it is mine!" he declared with villainous glee.

At that very moment, Batman and heroes Batwoman and Nightwing were on patrol in the Batplane.

"Alarms just went off at the museum," Batwoman said, checking the jet's computers.

"Let's go," Batman replied.

"You're not taking that scroll anywhere," Batman declared to the well-dressed man after the heroes rushed into the museum.

"I must have this scroll," the man replied. "I must have the information it contains. You know who I am, Batman. I am Rā's al Ghūl!" Then, after a gesture from him, the ninjas attacked!

The heroes flew into battle, dodging the ninjas' sharp swords. The black-clad warriors were highly skilled, but they were no match for Batman and his friends.

The heroes fought valiantly until all the fierce ninjas were defeated.

Unfortunately, their leader had slipped away during the fight—with the scroll!

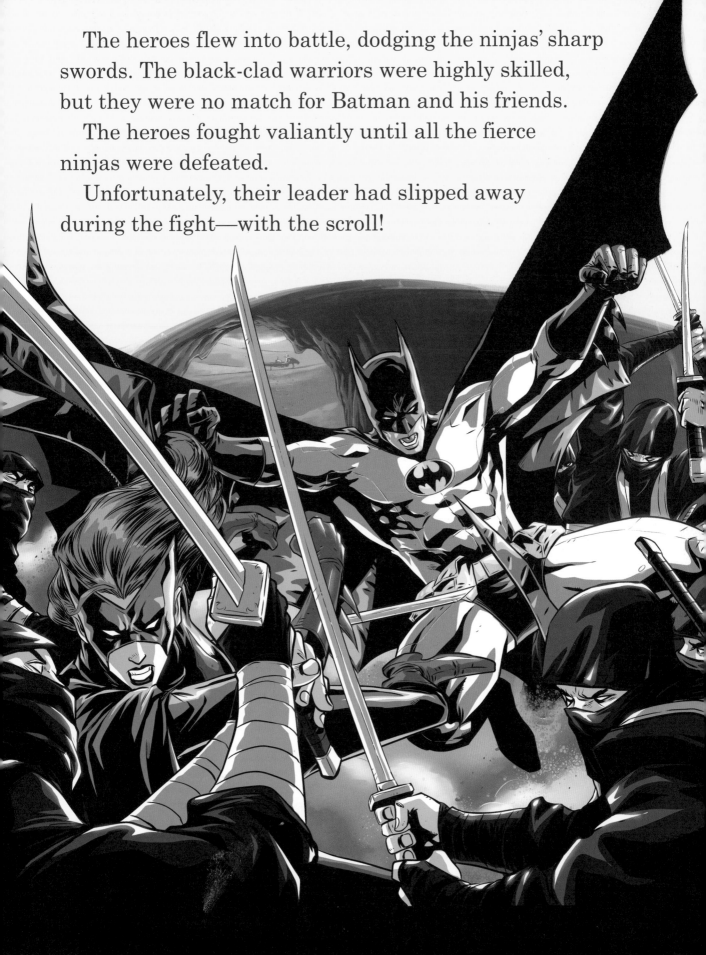

After the ninjas were taken away by the police,
the heroes assessed the situation.

"So, who is this Rā's al Ghūl?" Batwoman asked.

"And why does he want that scroll so badly?"
Nightwing added.

Batman pulled up the villain's files.

"The scroll supposedly shows the location of a fountain of youth," he explained. "Rā's al Ghūl is an old foe of mine. His greatest desire is to live forever. Luckily, in my other identity as Bruce Wayne, I made a computer copy of the scroll before he donated it to the museum. I know where he's headed. Let's go!"

While the heroes raced to find Rā's al Ghūl, the villain was
preparing to enter the fountain as his henchmen watched.
"Immortality will soon be mine," he said, his voice echoing
off the walls of the cave that sat deep in the earth.

"Not if I can help it,"
Batman said as he lassoed
Rā's al Ghūl with a Batrope.
"How dare you!" the villain roared.

Batwoman and Nightwing fought hard. Rā's al Ghūl's hulking henchman punched a wall, and the whole cave began to tremble!

CLANG! CLANG! CLANG!

Rā's al Ghūl leaped at Batman with a sword. Batman blocked the blade with two Batarangs. The sword and the Batarangs clashed again and again and again. The hero didn't want to hurt the villain, but he had to be stopped.

Rā's al Ghūl continued to fight Batman with the sword, but the hero quickly disarmed him.

"It's over, Rā's," Batman said as the cave crumbled.

"We have to go," Batwoman said. She and Nightwing helped the henchmen toward the exit.

"I won't be stopped! Immortality will be mine! I will live forever!" Rā's al Ghūl yelled, running back into the cave through the falling rubble.

"No," Batman cried out to his old foe, but it was too late. They were going to have to keep moving to escape.

"Do you think that's the last we've seen of Rā's al Ghūl?" Nightwing asked as the Batplane carried them home.

"It will take more than a cave-in to stop him," Batman replied. "A villain as determined as Rā's al Ghūl will be back. I'm sure of it."

ENTER THE RIDDLER

Some of the most important people in Gotham City were gathered at Wayne Manor to honor Commissioner Gordon. Just as Bruce Wayne handed him an award, an unexpected guest pushed his way to the stage. . . .

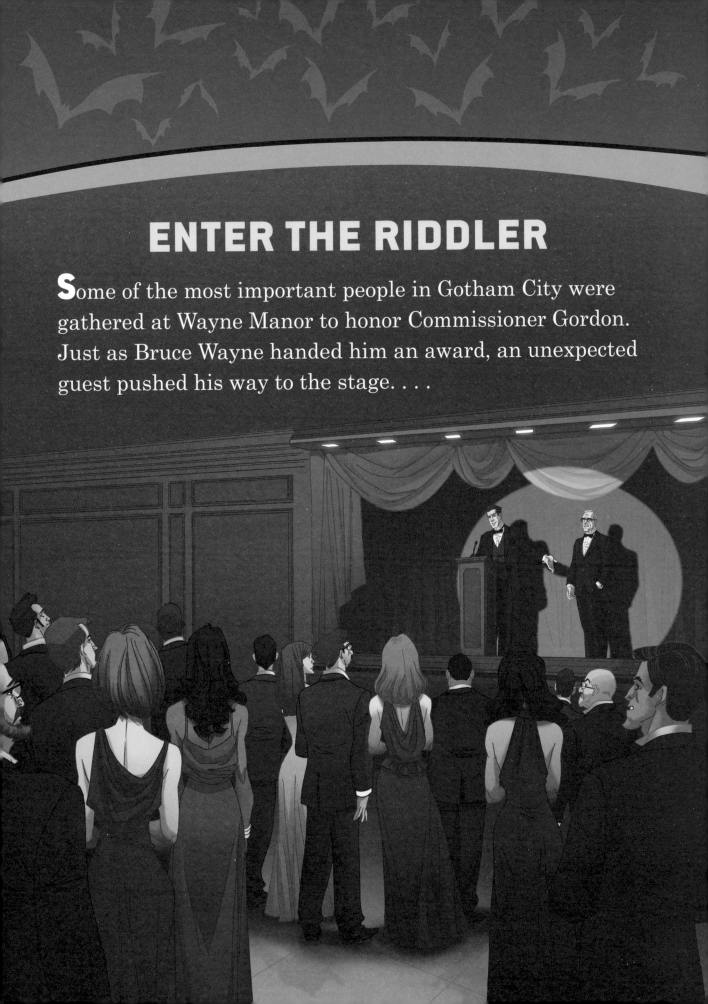

THE RIDDLER!

He grabbed the commissioner and said to the crowd, "If Batman wants to rescue your beloved Commissioner Gordon, then he'll have to riddle me this: When is the best time to go shopping?"

And with that—
POOF!—there was an explosion
of green smoke. When the smoke cleared, Bruce
Wayne was alone onstage. The Riddler and the commissioner
were gone!

Without a moment to lose, Bruce Wayne raced off to become
his heroic alter ego . . .

. . . BATMAN!

To solve the riddle, the hero tried to think like the villain. "Hmm . . . the best time to shop is when there's a . . . sale. Or in this case, a *sail*," said Batman. "He must mean the city harbor—that's where the city's sailboats are kept."

At the harbor, Batman searched until he found a sailboat with another riddle scrawled on its sail.

WHERE DO FISH KEEP THEIR LOOT?

The more you take, the more you leave behind

Batman thought for a moment. "Money is kept in a bank. I've got it. A riverbank!" he exclaimed.

He raced over to the water's edge and found another puzzling riddle. It said, "The more you take, the more you leave behind."

The answer was easy for Batman. "Footsteps!"

Batman slipped on his night-vision goggles and looked around. He found a set of footprints and followed them into a tunnel that led to a room with a door. As soon as he stepped inside, the door slammed shut. He saw another clue, but he was also locked in!

The room began to fill up with the answer to the puzzle: water!

Batman was trapped, and the water was rising fast.

"I'd better think quickly," Batman said, feeling the cold water get higher and higher, "or I'm done for."

Just then, the door opened! The water rushed out. "Batgirl!" Batman said with surprise and delight. "I sure am glad to see you."

Batman was one of the few people who knew Batgirl's secret. She was Commissioner Gordon's daughter!

"I've been on my dad's trail ever since the Riddler took him," she said. "And luckily, that led me to you, too!"

They followed Batgirl's tracker to a dark hole in the ground. They lowered themselves into the hole on their Batropes.

The Riddler was waiting there for Batman. "What took you so long?" he said with a laugh. "And it looks like you brought a friend. Well, the more, the merrier!"

"Don't worry, Commissioner," Batgirl said. "We'll be right down."

"You rescue Gordon," Batman whispered. "I'll stop the Riddler."

"I've got one last puzzle for you," the villain said. "And it's a real shocker!"

The Riddler pointed his cane at the heroes and directed
a massive electrical bolt at them. They were barely able

The Riddler forgot that he was standing in water—
and that electricity and water do not mix. The electricity
hit it and shocked *him* instead of his foes!
"OWW!" the Riddler howled.

Before he could recover, Batgirl was putting a pair of Bat-Cuffs on him.

"Good work," Batman said. It took him mere moments to rescue Commissioner Gordon, but when he turned around, Batgirl was gone. Only the Riddler remained.

"Where did she go?" Commissioner Gordon asked.

Batman heard her Batcycle rev to life and speed off into the night. "That's one riddle we may never have the answer to.""

BATCAVE BATTLE

The super-strong villain known as Bane had arrived in Gotham City. He wanted to challenge the Caped Crusader.

"Meet me, Batman!" the towering man shouted. "Meet me and let's decide who is the greatest fighter, once and for all."

"I'm here, Bane," Batman said, swinging down on a Batrope. "But let's leave the good people of Gotham City out of this."

"Of course. This is between you and me," Bane replied. He flexed his massive muscles. He was ready to wrestle.

Bane swung at Batman again and again with his huge fists, but the Caped Crusader always managed to avoid them—though just barely.

The two adversaries now cautiously circled each other. "I will crush you!" Bane roared as he charged.

Batman slipped to the side and used a quick kick to send the furious villain crashing to the ground!

"Stay down, Bane," Batman said.

"My thoughts exactly," Bane replied with a chuckle.

To Batman's surprise, Bane pulled out a smoke bomb and threw it at his feet. A thick cloud billowed around them. Batman couldn't see for a few moments, so Bane was able to get away.

"He must have escaped down this manhole," Batman said. "But that's odd. That hothead seemed so eager to fight. And it's certainly not like him to run away."

Back in his secret lair, the Batcave, Batman searched the sewer maps to see where Bane could have gone. He didn't have any luck. It seemed that the villain had disappeared!

"I think you will find what you are looking for right here," rumbled a deep voice from behind the hero.

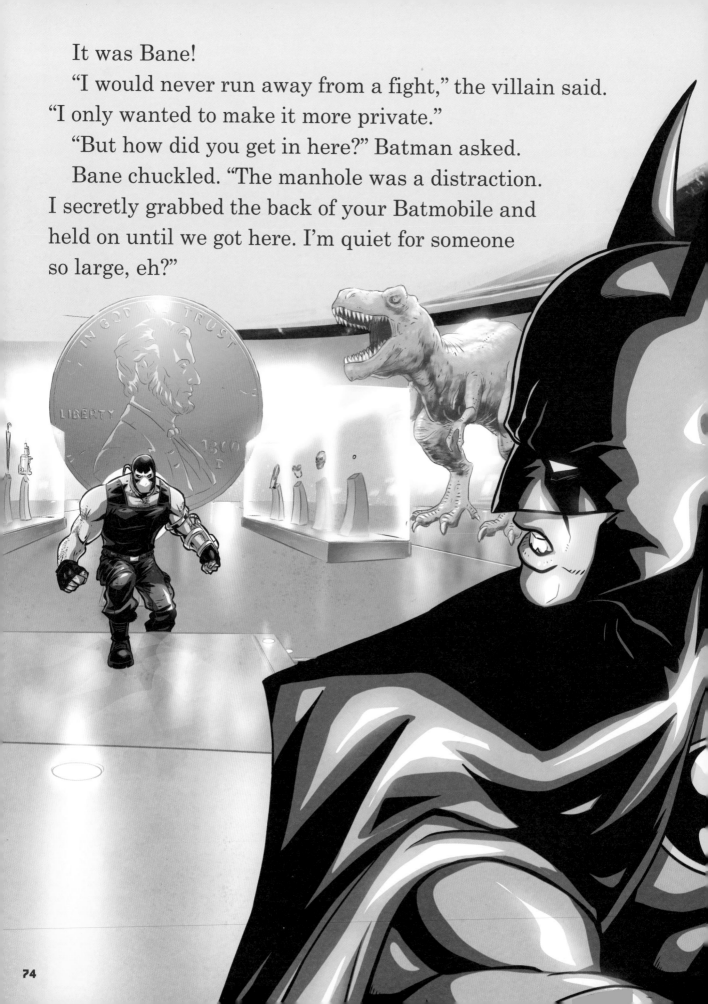

It was Bane!

"I would never run away from a fight," the villain said. "I only wanted to make it more private."

"But how did you get in here?" Batman asked.

Bane chuckled. "The manhole was a distraction. I secretly grabbed the back of your Batmobile and held on until we got here. I'm quiet for someone so large, eh?"

Batman turned to face his foe.
"Heads up, Caped Crusader!" Bane
grunted as he lifted the giant penny Batman
kept in the Batcave. "Today is not
your lucky day!"

Batman leaped into the air, barely avoiding
the huge coin as Bane sent it flying at him.
Meanwhile, Bane searched for another weapon.

He grabbed the villain Harley Quinn's giant mallet off the wall and charged at Batman. Bane swung the mallet again and again, but just as before, the hero was too fast for him.

"Sorry to interrupt, but I don't think you were invited," said a voice from behind Bane.

It was Robin, the Boy Wonder—Batman's trusted sidekick.

"If you want to use another villain's toy," Robin said with a smirk, "you should try something like . . ."

Robin fired the freeze ray, sealing Bane in a block of ice.

"Thanks, Robin," Batman said with a laugh. "Looks like you've taught Bane a good lesson about being coolheaded. Now let's get him to jail, where he belongs."

THE JOKER'S ICE SCREAM PARTY

It was the hottest day of the summer, and everyone in the Gotham City police station was sweating.

"We need something to cool us off," Commissioner Gordon said.

Through a window, he could hear the chimes of an ice cream truck outside.

"Perfect," he said. "Ice cream for everyone. My treat!"

Gotham City's finest lined up in front of the strange-looking green-and-purple truck to get a cold treat. No one noticed that the sign on the truck read ice *scream*, not ice cream.

A pale woman was serving the police force, and she giggled every time she handed out one of the frosty confections.

"It's so good, you just gotta laugh," she said, giggling again.

She wasn't kidding. After a few bites of the sweet treats, the officers began to laugh and laugh and laugh. They couldn't stop!

Inside the truck, the pale woman changed her outfit. She was really the villain Harley Quinn!

"You've tickled their taste buds, boss," Harley said as she leaned into the front seat of the truck. The driver was none other than the Joker!

"And with the cops being all giggles," he said, giggling himself, "Gotham City is ours for the taking. Hee, hee, hee!"

During Batman's patrol of the city in his Batmobile, he reached the police station and sensed that something was wrong. He noticed all the ice cream wrappers, cups, and cones on the ground.

With tools from his Utility Belt, he took samples and ran them through the Batmobile's computer. The results were not good! Not good at all.

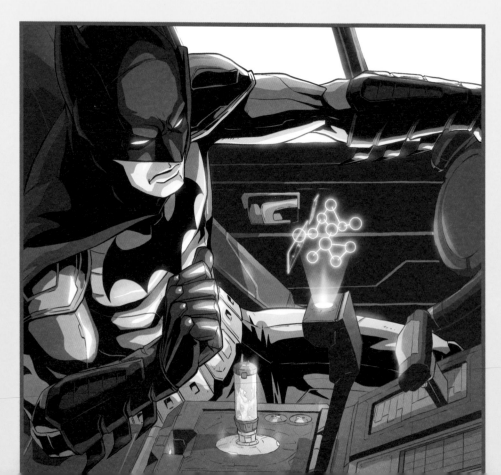

Batman called Batgirl. He told her that someone was serving ice cream to the police force that not only made them laugh uncontrollably but would also make them *eat* uncontrollably.

"They won't be able protect the city," Batgirl said.

"Exactly," Batman replied. "I'm on the trail of the suspects right now."

As Batman followed the ice cream truck, it transformed into a brightly colored buggy. It was the Jokermobile!

"Just as I suspected—the Joker!" Batman said. "Batgirl, follow the Batmobile's signal. I'm going to need your help with this one."

The Joker led Batman on a high-speed chase through the streets of Gotham City. But no matter how fast the criminal clown drove or how much he turned, swerved, and veered, he couldn't lose Batman.

"I'll take care of him lickety-split," said Harley, pressing some buttons on the dashboard of the Jokermobile. The wild-driving buggy started spewing chocolate syrup, cherries, bananas, and more at the Batmobile. Batman had to slow down in the sticky mess.

"Woo-hoo!" the Joker and Harley cheered. But just
when they thought they had gotten away, Batgirl roared
up the street ahead of them on her Batcycle. She threw
a Batarang right at the Jokermobile's front tire.

KA-POW! The tire popped, causing the buggy to come to a crashing halt and sticky ice cream to splatter all over the two villains. *Yuck!*

"Looks like these two have brain freeze," Batgirl said with a laugh.

"Help me take them and their buggy back downtown," Batman said. "They're going to get Gotham City out of the sticky situation they created."

Batman put an antidote in the remaining ice cream.
Then he and Batgirl stood guard while they made the Joker
and Harley serve it to the hungry police force. Before long,
everyone was back to normal.

"Now let's see how the Joker and Harley like serving time in jail," Batgirl said.

"Ha. Ha," the Joker said as he handed out another scoop. "Very funny."

"I call that just *desserts*," Batman replied as the villains and their buggy got hauled away.

POISON IVY'S PLANTS OF PERIL!

The people of Gotham City were enjoying a late-summer carnival. There were rides to go on, fun foods to enjoy, and events to attend. Children were running around, having a great time.

One of the events was a contest to see who could grow the largest fruits and vegetables.

"I think we have a winner," said one of the judges, who was standing in front of a very large pumpkin. The other judge held up the blue-ribbon prize.

But before the award could be given, the pumpkin split open.

CRACK!

"Hello, humans," said a plant-covered woman as she stepped out of the giant squash. It was the super-villain POISON IVY.

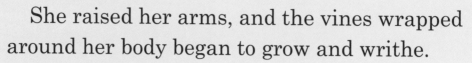

She raised her arms, and the vines wrapped around her body began to grow and writhe.

"How dare you turn these beautiful plants into oversized monstrosities just for your own amusement!" Poison Ivy roared.

The carnival-goers ran as the slithering vines went after them.

Commissioner Gordon was at the carnival with his daughter, Barbara.

"Get out of here!" he told her. "Call Batman. I'll try to slow Poison Ivy down until he gets here."

"Stop right there," the commissioner said to Poison Ivy in a deep, commanding voice. The villain just laughed. She knew he was no match for her plant powers. With only a thought, she made her vines wrap the commissioner up tightly and lift him into the air.

Barbara Gordon ran behind a tent. She alerted Batman with her wrist communicator that there was trouble. But she did more than that. When she was sure that no one could see her, she changed into her crime-fighting alter ego! Even her father didn't know that she was really **BATGIRL!**

The young super hero ran to meet up with the Caped Crusader.

"Let's untangle this mess before it grows any bigger," Batman said.

Using the sharp edges of their Batarangs, the two heroes cut through the knotty mass of vines, making their way to the super-villain.

"What's eating you this time, Poison Ivy?" Batman asked the villain as they got closer.

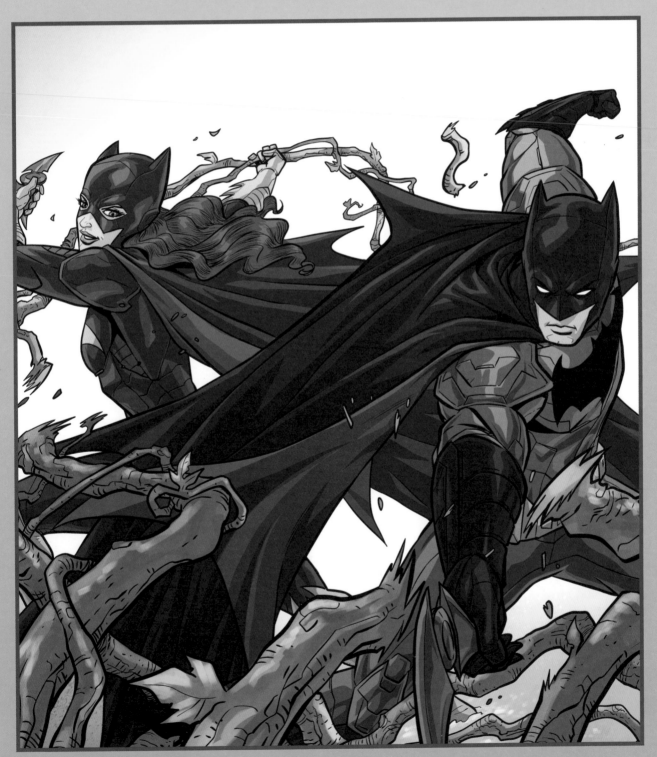

"I just can't stand by while humans use strange chemicals and fertilizers to harm my plant friends," Poison Ivy replied.

"Your intentions may be noble," Batgirl said, "but we can't let you hurt these people."

Just when she and Batman reached Poison Ivy, the shell of the giant pumpkin clamped down on them, snapping shut. The shell was a trap!

"Ha, ha, ha!" the villain laughed as she commanded the thick vines to lift the heroes into the air.

Inside the giant pumpkin, Batman stuck a
Bat-grenade into the wall of the fleshy pumpkin.
"Get behind your cape," Batman said.
"Gotcha!" Batgirl replied. "Our fireproof capes
will protect us."

KA-BOOM! The pumpkin flew apart, freeing Batman and Batgirl. The two heroes dropped to the ground, unharmed. "My pumpkin!" Poison Ivy yelled. Now she was *really* mad!

But it was too late for the super-villain. She was surrounded.

"Give up," Batman said. "This carnival caper is over."

The villain knew she'd lost. She made her vines retreat, and she let her human captives go free.

"Scaring people is no way to get them to change," Batman said to Poison Ivy.

"But perhaps I planted the *seed*," she replied. "And people will start thinking about how they treat my plant friends."

"I hope you're right," Batman said as Batgirl led the villain away.

THE ICE PACK!

Batman, protector of Gotham City, was in his secret lair. His powerful computer collected information from all over so he could keep an eye out for signs of criminal activity. At the moment, some very strange reports were coming in.

Even though it was summertime, the temperature outside seemed to be going *down*.

"The city is getting colder and colder," Batman said. "And now it's starting to snow! Not good. I'd better investigate."

Batman raced into the city in the Batmobile. He didn't have much trouble locating the source of the trouble—it was the ice-hearted villain known as **MR. FREEZE**.

"I hope you've dressed warmly, Batman," the villain said. "The city is about to get a lot colder."

Mr. Freeze fired his ice ray at Batman, and the hero flipped out of the way. The ray created a slab of ice where he had been standing a split second before. Suddenly, more blasts came from another direction. Batman dodged those as well—but barely!

FSSSSSS!

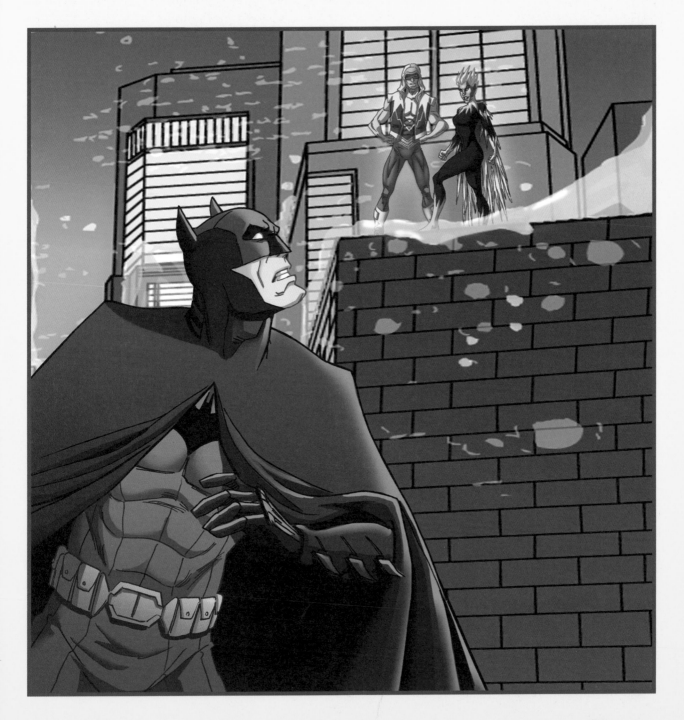

Batman looked up. Two more frosty felons were standing on a nearby rooftop.

"Captain Cold and Killer Frost," Batman said. "I should have known Mr. Freeze couldn't cause this much snow and ice alone."

"You got that right, Caped Crusader," Captain Cold replied. "We're gonna make a new ice age for Gotham City!"

Killer Frost and Captain Cold fired more blasts of
ice at Batman, and he dove into the Batmobile. The
armored vehicle protected the hero from the cold, but . . .

WHOOOSH!

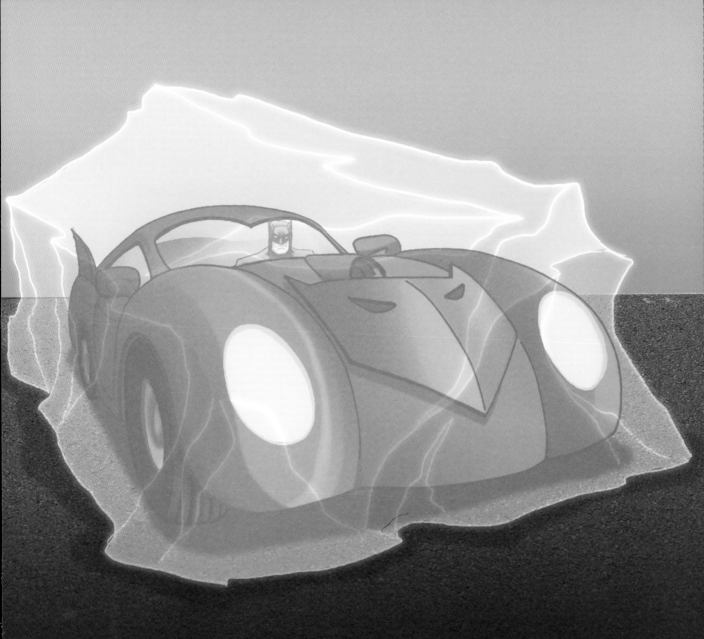

. . . the Batmobile was now encased in a block of ice.
Batman was trapped inside!

"I think I'm going to need to even the odds," he said.
"Three against one doesn't seem fair—especially with
their icy powers."

Batman pressed the emergency button on the car's controls. In seconds, a red-and-yellow blur appeared on his computer screen. It was . . .

...The Flash!

The Flash was known as the Fastest Man Alive. Super-speed was his superpower.

He ran circles around the Batmobile, creating a hot tornado that melted the ice.

"Be careful," Batman warned. "There are three of them."

"Don't worry," The Flash replied. "Wonder Woman is on her way."

Something whizzed past The Flash's head. He spun around in the blink of an eye to find Captain Cold firing cannonballs of rock-hard ice at him.

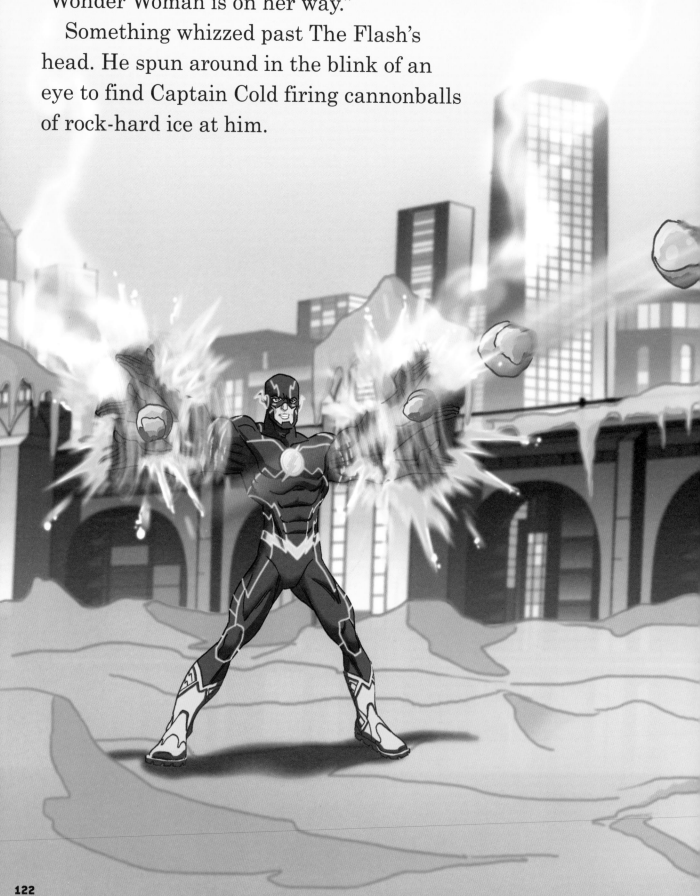

"You'll have to do better than that, Cold," the Scarlet Speedster said. The Flash twirled his arms at super-speed, creating a blurry red shield. The snowballs bounced harmlessly away from their target!

The Amazon warrior Wonder Woman arrived and immediately leaped into the battle. Killer Frost fired super-sharp icicles at her, but Wonder Woman used her amazing reflexes and unbreakable silver bracelets to deflect them.

"You'll have to be faster than that to freeze me," Wonder Woman said.

Despite their valiant efforts, the three super
heroes found themselves surrounded by the villains.
"We're going to get frozen if we don't come up
with a plan," Wonder Woman said.

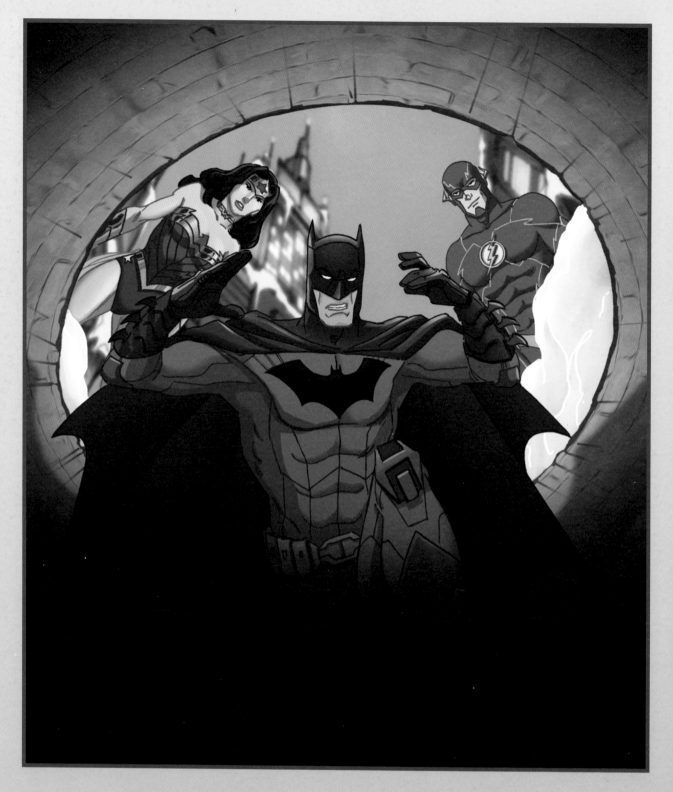

Batman spotted a manhole cover nearly
buried in the snow.

"Follow me," the Caped Crusader said to his
friends. He quickly told them his plan as they
disappeared into the darkness below.

The three villains followed the heroes into the tunnels, but a block away, they found only Batman.

"Ha! Looks like your friends gave you the cold shoulder," Mr. Freeze gloated.

"Actually, they're planning on warming things up," Batman said as he fired his grappling hook through a manhole above him and quickly made his escape.

Aboveground, Wonder Woman sealed the
manhole cover behind Batman while The Flash
raced around the city streets. The heat generated
by his super-speed melted the villains' ice and snow.

The water from the big melt flowed down into the tunnel.
"Do they really think this will stop us?" Mr. Freeze
growled as water rose around them.

But the rapidly rising water caused Mr. Freeze's ice
blaster to short-circuit. His powerful tech turned on him
and his partners.

The water suddenly froze! The ice-cold villains found themselves frozen in a block of ice. And to make matters worse, their frigid powers were making the water freeze even faster. They were stuck!

Wonder Woman used her super-strength to rip up the manhole cover to reveal the trapped criminals.

"Thank you," Batman said to his friends. "You helped me save Gotham City. I can take it from here."

"You got that right," The Flash joked. "Mr. Freeze and his frosty friends aren't going anywhere—until all that ice melts."

"We're happy to help," Wonder Woman said as she took to the sky.

"And I'll use my super-speed to clean up the rest of this snow and ice on my way out of town," The Flash added, becoming a red blur as he raced away.

Later that day, Batman relaxed at home as Bruce Wayne. His butler, Alfred, handed him a glass of iced tea.

"Actually," Bruce Wayne joked, "I think I'd like my tea to be *hot* today."

THE CAT AND THE CLOWNS!

As night fell, billionaire Bruce Wayne walked down the stairs to a large hidden cavern beneath his mansion. It was the secret lair of his crime-fighting alter ego . . .

"There appears to be some trouble in downtown Gotham City, sir," said his butler, Alfred, checking Batman's crime-fighting computer. "Some alarms have gone off around the city. And then there's this. . . ."

Alfred showed Batman something on the screen.

"The Bat-Signal is already shining over the city," the butler said.

"It must something too big for the police to handle," Batman replied. "Don't stay up—it looks like I may be working late tonight."

Batman pulled his mask over his head and double-checked his Utility Belt. The belt contained everything he needed for his work as the World's Greatest Detective.

Batman jumped into the rocket-powered Batmobile and roared into the night. He headed straight for Gotham City.

Inside the Batmobile, the video screen lit up. It was Commissioner Gordon.

"There's something going on at the art museum," the commissioner said. "I sent some police officers over there a while ago, but I've lost contact with them."

"Don't worry," Batman said. "I'm on my way."

"There's a rare-jewels exhibit at the museum," Batman said to himself as he ran up the front stairs of the museum. "They're worth a fortune. And there are any number of criminals who would love to get their hands on them."

Just as he'd suspected, a crime was in progress. The front door had been smashed in, and the guards and police were nowhere to be found.

Inside the museum, Batman saw one of the guards tied up. He raced over to help him, but he realized too late that it was a trap! A net fell over the Caped Crusader.

"*Purr*-fect," said Catwoman. The famous feline cat burglar was not alone: the Riddler and the Joker were there, too. They had teamed up to rob the museum.

"That's quite a catch, Catwoman," the Joker said with a laugh.

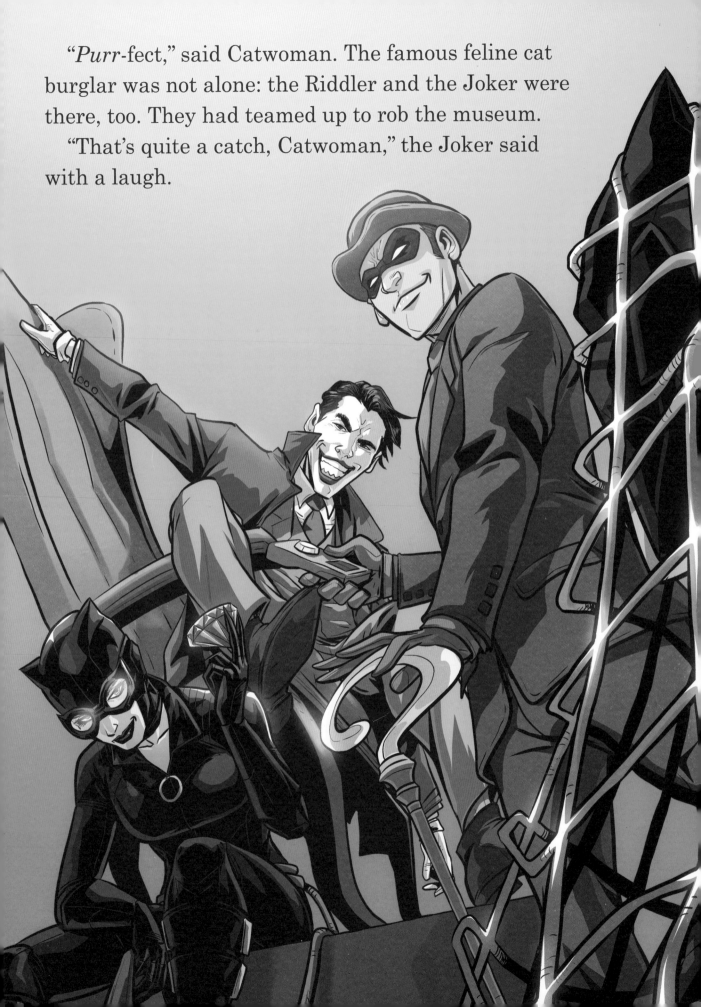

As the villains started to leave with the museum's precious jewels, Batman cut his way through the net with a Batarang. Then the hero threw the Batarang at the Riddler.

"Arrgh!" the villain cried as the twirling weapon hit his bag, spilling the stolen gems onto the floor. Before he could make a move, Batman slapped Bat-Cuffs on his wrists.

Catwoman and the Joker had already escaped, so Batman untied the guards and left the Riddler with them.

"Tell Commissioner Gordon I'm on the trail of the other two," Batman said as he raced into the night.

"You got it, Batman," replied one of the guards.

Batman caught up with the two villains, but the Joker had leaped into a helicopter and was escaping with his henchmen.

"I hope you have nine lives!" the Joker yelled as he left Catwoman behind to flee on foot. "Toodle-oo!"

Batman wasn't going to let the clown get away that easily. He threw a magnetic tracer that stuck to the Joker's helicopter.

"I'll be seeing you later," Batman muttered. "But first—Catwoman."

Batman chased Catwoman to the Gotham City waterfall. The rushing water was too rough to cross, and the falls were too high for even the criminal cat to climb. She was trapped. She had no choice but to give up.

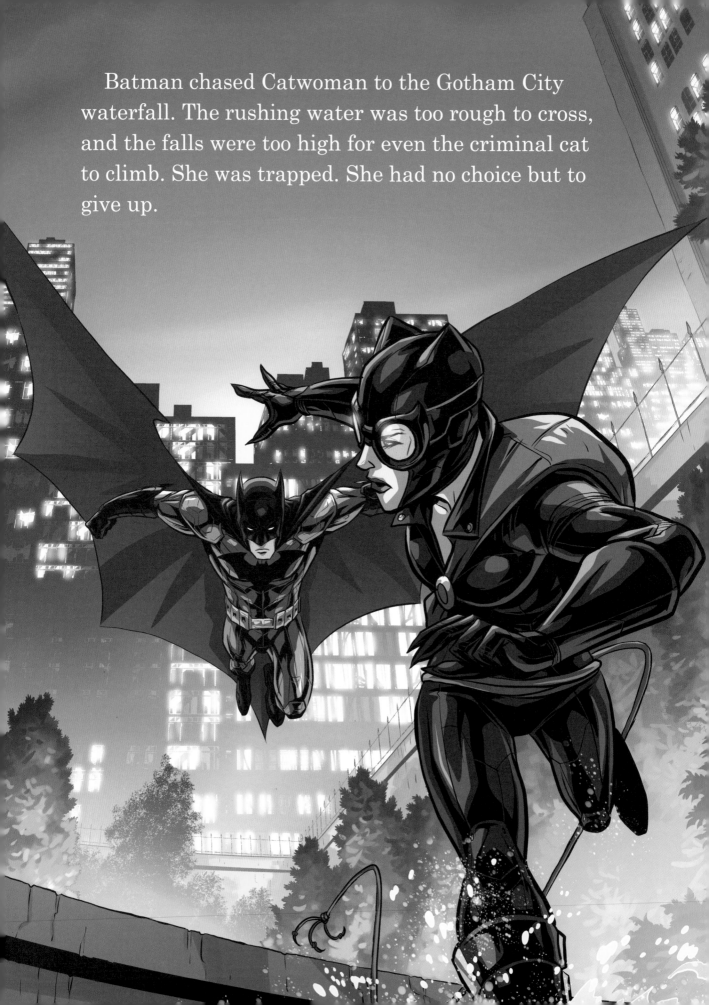

Batman used his second pair of Bat-Cuffs
to secure Catwoman until the police arrived.

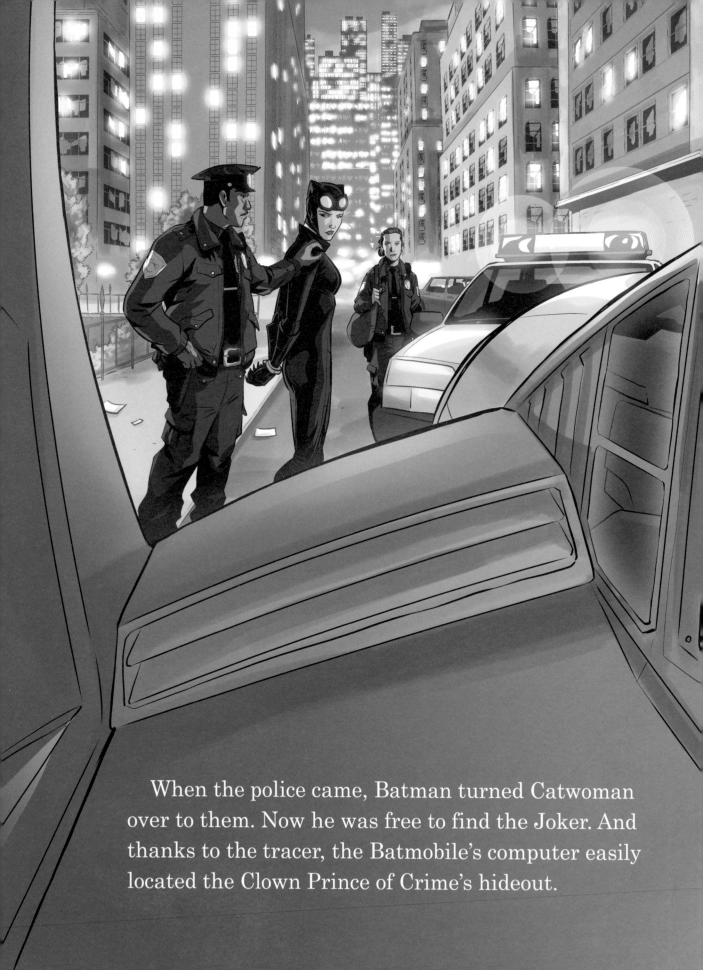

When the police came, Batman turned Catwoman over to them. Now he was free to find the Joker. And thanks to the tracer, the Batmobile's computer easily located the Clown Prince of Crime's hideout.

He sent the coordinates to Commissioner
Gordon so the police could meet him there.
"Let's end this night with a laugh," Batman
told the commissioner via video link as the
Batmobile roared off into the night.

The Joker and his henchmen were celebrating in their hideout. The jewels the Joker had stolen were going to make them rich!

The Joker giggled gleefully. "For once, we got away from that do-gooder—

BATMAN!"

The Caped Crusader came crashing through the skylight. The villains and his henchmen scattered. The criminal clown tried to grab some of the jewels in hopes of making another daring escape.

Batman rounded up the motley crew of criminals
and quickly secured them with a Batrope.
"Just like the bow on a birthday present, I'd say
you are all tied up," Batman said to the Joker.

The police arrived a few minutes later. They would take the crooks to jail and return the stolen jewels to the museum.

"Thank you, Batman," Commissioner Gordon said. "With that trio of troublemakers behind bars, Gotham City is safe again."

Batman disappeared into the night. Gotham City might be safe for the moment, but the hero knew it would only stay that way as long as he was there to protect it.